PELICULA

A hundred years or so ago a novelist didn't have to deify the visual medium, but today, oh if you don't, the goddess of cinema will become enraged.

-Frank Cherbourg

PRELUDE

'Wolfgang. What's this book about?'

'It's a story about a young and beautiful actress named Katherine Whitaker. A household name not quite yet, she's been working steadily in movies and TV since she was sixteen. But now here she is, twenty-four, and her time has finally come. She's been tapped to star in a big-budget Hollywood blockbuster, based on an already best-selling adventure video game entitled Uber Girl. Three months before shooting is to begin, the contracts have been signed, ads have gone out in the trades, Katherine, while training for the role, one day discovers she's pregnant. Holy shit, what is to be done? Should the baby be aborted so Katherine can go on to play Uber Girl? A role that will change her life and career forever. Or should she say yes to a role much more complex: That of motherhood? Now don't be alarmed if what you read at first seems totally unrelatable to what this book is about. The novel's shocking twist at the end will make you realize that the journey that just preceded you had every reason to play out exactly as it did.'

'Wolfgang rock on. Rock on my friend.'

'Who are you and why do you ask me a question like this?' she queried. The voice did not answer her, but instead asked another question.

'But whom is your impending marriage really for? Is it for you? Or are you doing it to meet the expectations of those whom you love?' This sudden remonstrance had done the expected to her: It had thrown her into a state of great upheaval.

'You will see nothing but total darkness, very shortly,' said the voice. 'Don't be alarmed. You're only going to faint.'

'But our little talk?'

'To be continued,' answered the voice. 'To be continued.'

Had she done the right thing in stopping the wedding? Not everyone was agreeable of course. Mom especially.

'What will everyone think?' she kept going on. 'What will everyone think?'

'What do I care what other people think?'

Her mother was at an end. 'I can see that it's going to be pointless for me to argue this out any further . . . Oh! . . . To tell you the truth, Pelicula, if I were your age and I were given the chance to do it all over again, I'd have done what you just did.'

realize that the journey that just preceded you had every reason to play out exactly as it did.'

'Wolfgang rock on. Rock on my friend.'

1

Off went the light in the bathroom and towards the main floor of her apartment Pelicula was now moving. She looked absolutely beautiful. Her sandy blonde hair, recently washed and fragrant with the smell of hyacinth and honey, had been freed from its usual ponytail and was now unfurling past the nape of her neck, to the tips of her shoulders. She'd applied makeup, and had now changed from jeans and a t-shirt, into a pink summer dress, which she'd bought earlier that afternoon at her favorite boutique.

'He'll find you irresistible in that,' said the saleslady.

'You think?'

'You won't even get through dinner.'

She began to reflect on the experience once more. 'He'll find you irresistible in that . . . He'll find you irresistible in that . . . Of course he will,' she exclaimed! And what shot immediately through her body was a tingle of excitement. Slowing her walk, she repeated these words once more, and straight away what sprouted in her mind was this idea that, as of late, had begun to turn up ever so frequently. That was, that very soon she'd be performing the one role she'd always longed to play in this life: That of a baby maker.

Rounding a corner, she stepped onto a boulevard. The sun was beginning to fade and she knew it was only a matter of time before the afternoon would be taken away from her.

'Soon there will be so few afternoons left for you,' said a voice in her head. 'You'll wake up one day and realize that it all went and went very quickly, in the blink of an eye. What is it that you are doing with your life, young lady? What is it that you are doing?'

Her walk had come to an abrupt halt. She could feel her eyelids flickering and thought that their rapidity was almost equal in rhythm to her beating heart.

'Who are you and why do you ask me a question like this?' she queried. The voice did not answer her, but instead asked another question.

'But whom is your impending marriage really for? Is it for you? Or are you doing it to meet the expectations of those whom you love?' This sudden remonstrance had done the expected to her: It had thrown her into a state of great upheaval.

'You will see nothing but total darkness, very shortly,' said the voice. 'Don't be alarmed. You're only going to faint.'

'But our little talk?'

'To be continued,' answered the voice. 'To be continued.'

Had she done the right thing in stopping the wedding? Not everyone was agreeable of course. Mom especially.

'What will everyone think?' she kept going on. 'What will everyone think?'

'What do I care what other people think?'

Her mother was at an end. 'I can see that it's going to be pointless for me to argue this out any further . . . Oh! . . . To tell you the truth, Pelicula, if I were your age and I were given the chance to do it all over again, I'd have done what you just did.'

'But then I'd never have been born.'

Her mother looked into her daughter's eyes.

'How did Jonathan react when you told him?'

'He didn't say much. I think he was more shocked than anything.'

Her mother shook her head. 'Men are never shocked when an engagement is broken off. Relieved maybe, but never shocked.'

Her mother looked at her daughter once more.

'And so what do you make of all this pain you've caused me?'

'I'm sorry, but is it really much compared to what I would have had to go through had I gotten married.'

Her mother screwed up her gaze.

'You're being a little selfish, aren't you?'

'I'm only doing what you wished you would've done. Did you, at twenty-two, really want to get married and start having kids? I think not. You only did it because grandma pressured you into it. Just like her mother did, and her mother did . . . and so on . . . and so on . . . But none of you women ever had the courage to stand up and say, maybe this is not what I want!'

Her mother drew back.

'Your father said that you were also dropping out of University?'

'That is correct.'

'But you're only a year away from finishing?'

'I'm finished now.'

Her mother threw up her hands.

'Can you not stop and think about someone other than yourself for a moment?'

'But I did that. And it made me very unhappy.'

Her mother took exception to this.

'And what about my unhappiness?'

'That is for you to figure out.'

She would do as she pleased, then, it was settled, and not only in her mind, but in the minds of others.

'Wow,' said her best friend Anna K, to her, the next morning. 'I really wish I could go around telling people to go fuck themselves.'

'That's not exactly how it went.'

'I don't care how it went. You're my hero.'

Pelicula gave this some thought.

'If it's true that society is made up of a great majority of people who have almost *no* spare money and then of a small minority of people who have *way* too much spare money, why did I give up the chance to belong to this club of the have it all's?'

'I didn't know Jonathan's family was that rich?'

Pelicula nodded.

'Then you are either incredibly smart. Or incredibly fuckin stupid.'

Pelicula laughed.

'Maybe you're saying it's better if we don't analyze it.'

Her friend thought for a second and then shook her head.

'No . . . No, I think we should. Because I find what you did very interesting.'

'I made a decision that wasn't cash based.'

'And that's very unusual, because most people in your position would've gotten married anyway. Taken the money. Especially those coming from such a modest upbringing as yours.'

Her friend then lit a cigarette, which Pelicula thought very strange because she had no recollection of ever having seen her smoke.

'What do you have there, in your bag?' her friend asked.

Pelicula looked flustered.

'Oh . . . these? They're . . . They're just some things I've been writing down. I've been having some strange dreams lately.'

'Dreams? It looks like you've put them into some sort of diary journal, story form?'

Pelicula nodded.

'May I read some of it?'

Pelicula handed the diary over and her friend took a look.

'*And so last night I dreamt once again that I was a man. . . .*'

Her friend looked up.

'You dreamt that you were a man?! How incredible! How absolutely incredible! I've never had a dream like that and I've always wondered what it would be like to have one.'

I was asking someone where I could get something to eat. A small boy, thin and tanned, and speaking in English that was broken, pointed me towards a tiny cafe just a block to my left. As I was walking away he asked me a question that was straight forward enough: He asked me if I needed a girl. Because he said that he could get me one. One very beautiful, that would keep good company for a nice-looking gentleman like me. He was smiling so happily, I remember, right before he walked away, and I couldn't recall whether I'd told him I wanted one or not.

And so it wasn't long before I realized that I was in some foreign country like say in Africa, or something, but I couldn't be sure, because this was a dream and in dreams you can never be sure of anything.

'Do you think the same can be said about life?'
'But life isn't like a dream?'
'It isn't?'

And so maybe a fraction of a second after my meal was eaten a very young, good-looking woman began propositioning me in the kinkiest sort of way.

'If you come with me handsome man, I can make some very good fun for you. I think zat you would like dat, wouldn't you, handsome man? For me to make lots of za fun for you.'

'Were you in Europe?'

'Like I said Africa . . . I think. But the prostitute was Dutch, looked like a movie star . . . Oh, I don't know . . . Can't be sure.'

'No worries. Let us go back.'

By now some time had passed and I had yet to tell the woman whether or not I was up for it. This wasn't a play on my part. I was just trying to get to know her better.

'How much did you say this fun would cost me?'

'100 dollars.'

'1 dollar?'

'No . . . One . . . Hundred . . . Dollars. One, zero, zero.' And she held up her fingers in the shape of these numbers.

'Oh, I see.'

'So does zee man vant to come with me or not?'

'What? Am I no longer handsome?'

'Ahh . . . Fuuu.'

'But I don't even know your name? Marlene Dietrich can't be your real name.'

'Ahh . . . Zeeenough of you!' And she got up to leave, but not before I was able to hand her a little money.

'For your time,' I said.

A man had tried strangling her several days ago, she told me, a soldier guy, and had almost killed her. This happens quite a lot, she said.

'Why do you do it?' I asked. 'You said that you don't really like the sex.'

'Because the money is so good,' she replied. 'I am za slave to za money.'

'But you know you can't do this for the rest of your life.'

'No. I know. But I am zaving up zeenough to get zout of here. To get zout of here! And make nice baby. Dat is my dream. To do dat.'

'I knew a man who worked 'just for the money' at a miserable job for years. Hated it and everyday he swore he would one day leave. Opportunities came and went, but for some reason or another he never took them. Finally, no more opportunities came, and he was dead. That was his life. If this happens to you young lady, I'll shoot you. Do you hear that? I'll shoot you. Have you ever heard the saying . . . If you can't do it today, what's to say that you're going to be able to do it tomorrow? Does this make any sense to you?'

'Yes Handsome Man.'

'Good. I think everyone should have dreams, and I wish you much luck in moving in on yours.'

'Nice baby. I vant to make.'

INTERIOR BUILDING - DAY. PELICULA'S MOM: A SHORT Q&A.

'Tell me about yesteryear? You studied as an actress before you gave birth to Pelicula is that right?'

'I studied for a year.'

'And what was that experience like?'

'Crazy. My teacher was a lunatic.'

13

'Did you learn how to act?'

'I think the only way to likely learn anything is to just do it. Especially when it comes to something creative. If you want to be an actor, go out and act. If you want to be a painter, go out and paint. If you want to be a writer, go out and write. Most teachers in the creative profession are just trying to make money off your insecurities anyway. They're a bunch of failures, for the most part, who've never actually done the thing which you yourself are trying to do. So why would you want to hang around a person like that? What sort of inspiration are you going to get from a loser and a con artist? This is why I didn't ball my eyes out when Pelicula told me she wouldn't be finishing university. I think it's probably the best thing for her.'

'Did you tell her that?'

'No. It's impossible for me to tell her the complete truth of how I feel just yet.'

'Why?'

'I don't know.'

'She was studying writing, correct?'

'Yes.'

'Let's talk about your husband. He had aspirations to be a professional pianist?'

'Yes he did. But when Pelicula was born I told him to shelve them and get a real job.'

'And did he?'

'Of course. What choice did he have?'

'And what did he end up doing?'

'He ended up teaching music at a high school.'

So after a few minutes had passed, my waitress came out.

'*I'm sorry that prostitute was bothering you Handsome Man. I wanted to tell her to leave, but I wasn't sure if you wanted to go with her or not.*'

'*I'm not sure myself what it was that I wanted from her.*'

'*My name is Joan. Joan Crawford.*'

'*My name is Pelicula.*'

'*Pelicula? That is a very strange name for a man? It sounds French. Is it French?*'

'*I'm not sure where it comes from?*'

INTERIOR HOUSE - LATE IN THE EVENING: JONATHAN ON THE PHONE, WHILST STILL REELING.

'Dude . . . Dude are you up?'

'Jonathan? What's going on bro?'

'You sound like you're sleeping?'

'No man, I'm sentient. What up?'

'Dude check this out . . . Pelicula called me about half an hour ago and she was like on fire.'

'What?'

'The chick was freakin out man. Like saying all this wack shit.'

'Like what?'

'Dude . . . She said she's been having these crazy dreams where she's like a man.'

'Get out . . . And she told you this?'

'Yeah . . . And the guy is like really good lookin so all these chicks are like wanting to ride him.'

'No way bro that is awesome.'

'And check this out . . . She's all like hyper and stuff on the phone, like cryin and saying shit like, I had a dream last night where I could've fucked a whore if I wanted to, but I didn't because I thought about you.'

'I could've fucked a whore if I wanted to, but I didn't because I thought about you . . . Man that sounds like a country western song.'

'I know. I know it does. And so then after the whore leaves she starts going off about how her and this waitress named Joan Crawford start talking about all sorts of girl shit. . . .'

'Like what? Oprah, Ellen and shopping n' stuff?'

'I don't know . . . probably. So eventually we find out that this Joan girl has a brother named Mickey Rooney.'

'Mickey Rooney?'

'And that this guy Mickey has just lost his managerial job at this nickel mine that my old man now owns.'

'Your dad just bought it from that country's government.'

'That's right.'

'Woe. Which country was it?'

'I don't know. Some third world African country I guess.'

'Wow. That's some crazy shit, man. That's some crazy shit . . . But let me tell you what I think.'

'What?'

'That this chick still totally wants to hump you.'

'Do you think?'

'No doubt about it man. No doubt at all. I'll say that this chick still totally wants to hump you. She does.'

Anna picked up the diary once again, about a week later.

'You've written something down here about Jonathan and his buddy Cornilieus T. Tashman.'

'I just put it in the other night.'

'May I read it?'

'Be my guest.'

Jonathan is 6'1, has jet-black curly hair, sexy green eyes and dark skin. His race is mixed you would say. Cornilieus is close to him in height, but probably a little shorter, with blonde hair, blue eyes, and a healthy, white complexion. Without a doubt, their physicality makes you feel hopeful for humanity. Too bad their level of maturity doesn't.

And so at forty-two, her mother had made the decision to go back to acting.

'Are you going into the theatre then?'

Her mother frowned at the suggestion.

'The theatre? My god are you kidding? If any form of art has become the world's biggest novelty in the last hundred years it's live theatre. It really has. Ask someone how many plays they've seen in the last year or two? None, or maybe one, because some guy was on a date and he wanted to show his girl how 'cultured' he was so he took her to the theatre, hoping to get a little pussy in the end. No, I think people are generally bored when they go to the theatre nowadays because it's so hard for them to relate to the medium anymore. And why? Because they've grown so accustomed to a form of catharsis that is so preeminent for the 21st century: The electronic screen. Film screens, television screens, computer screens, iPhone screens, iPad screens, cell phone screens, this screen gadget screen, whatever screen gadget screen you have, big or small, or from whatever medium. Its very nature just mesmerizes us in such away that the theatre never did. There's just something about it.

Imagine it's around 1917, and you've never before been to see a movie. You're sixteen years old. That afternoon your parents tell you that they're taking you to see a couple of plays. One tonight and then another tomorrow. Like a lot of people who live in a city like yours, you maybe see a few a week, maybe more, so this isn't a big deal. It's just nice to get out of the house because there's no television at home, Instagram or Facebook, to keep you from being bored. So that evening you go to see a performance of something written by a guy named Shaw. It's entertaining enough, something about a prostitute and the defects of modern capitalism. Okay great. Liked it. And so the next day you go to see something by this dude named Strindberg. It's about some rich chick who gets it on with her male servant.'

'Well I liked that one even before I saw it. . . .'

'You say to your folks. As you're leaving the theatre, your father tells you that these two dudes Strindberg and Shaw are big men with big ideas, and that they make the theatre great. You suddenly remember something someone said to you just the other day.'

'Did you know, father, that someone told me that in a 100 years or so the theatre will become something of a horse and pony show for people? That there won't be much of an audience for it anymore, and that these guys Strindberg and Shaw will have to learn to do something else, like write for the movies. . . .'

'And your father stops you right there.'

'Now listen! If I ever hear you saying such things about the theatre again, my god, I will take a strap to your ass and whip it until it has bled to a devil red! Do you hear me?! Do you hear me?! And never! Never, ever let me catch you in a movie house! Is that understood?! They are full of lowlifes

20

and degenerates. If you want real art you go to the theatre. If you want filth you go to a movie house! Understand?'

'Yes sir.'

'But what if Young Man? What if you want to piss off your parents and you go to a movie anyways? I want the people of 1917 to know that what they're staring at will one day become the most powerful preceptor that the world has ever known, and likely will ever know. This screen will teach and train you how to do almost everything: How to talk, how to dress, what to drink, what to eat, how to cheat, how to steal, how to live, how to learn, how to lie, how to kill, how to blow things up, how to moralize, what to feel, and how to fuck. You will one day be unable to escape from these screens. They'll be everywhere. In almost every room in your home, at your workplaces, in your fitness centers, at the dentist's office, in your hospitals, at airports, in your schools, on airplanes, in cars, inside bathrooms, at the mechanics, in the hair salon, at the brothel. Help! Help! I'm lost in a forest! Oh, don't worry, you can still keep yourself busy by watching a movie. So have fun 1917 people! Have fun! But hang on! Because everything is about to change! And change fast!'

INTERIOR FILM SET - PRESENT DAY: THE MISFITS OF THE WORLD, OH HOW THEY DO PLAY.

'All right cut. Awesome take! Print it!'

'What a fuckin performance big guy. You nailed it!'

'Thanks.'

'Okay check the gate in the camera. If the gate's good, we're moving on.'

'The gate's good.'

'All right, then. New deal. Relax the actors and bring in their Stand-ins so we can set up for the next shot.'

'Where's Wolfgang?'

'He's outside.'

'Bring him in.'

'Copy that.'

'What do I do with the extras?'

'The extras? You can send them back to holding.'

'Extras you can go back to holding.'

'What about our props?'

'Your props? Hold on. Let me see . . . Stevie? Stevie go to 2.'

Some silence ensues, then, into his walkie again.

'Stevie where do the extras leave their props?'

He nods. Nods again.

'On the table. Okay. Copy that. On the table. You extras can leave your props over there on the table.'

'Bring in 2nd team. The Stand-ins? Where the hell are they?'

Silence ensues. The man, his patience has collapsed.

'Those dopey fuckin dumb Stand-ins?! Will someone go out and get them pleeeease!'

2

Yes. It's true. The woman you're about to meet is nuts. Pretty darn nuts, yes.

3

INT. AUTHOR'S STUDY - MORNING
A YOUNG WOMAN (24-26) sits in her ONE ROOM
APARTMENT writing on a computer. The place is
clean, but scarce.

So hey there Valued Reader what do you think
of this book so far? Are you liking it? What about
these characters, eh? Are you digging them? Do you
like Pelicula and her friend Anna K? I do. What's the
word on the street about this Handsome Man guy?
Do people think he's groovy? Or do they think he's
just a big wanker? Or how about that whore he was
talking to, Marlene, I think her name was. I wonder
if she'll ever leave the whoring life like she says she
will. Who else is there? Oh, there's a waitress named
Joan, but we didn't find out too much about her, did
we? And how about those two good lookin rich
boys? The ex-fiancé, Jonathan, and his buddy

25

Cornilieus T. Tashman. What a couple of party boy hosers they seem to be. And let's not forget Pelicula's kooky mother. What can you say about a woman who wants to be an actress again after twenty years of being away from it? And what about that voice in Pelicula's head? I liked that and got really excited when that happened, but if we don't hear from it again, I won't sweat it. And I hope you won't either, Valued Reader.

So anyways, I'm this book's author, Madeline Macdonald. And what else does a girl who's never, ever, written a book before have to say? That she's never, ever, read very many of them neither. You see, books have never interested me that much. And to be honest with you I don't think books nowadays interest a whole lot of people that much. Especially ones like this that are considered fiction. Whatever that's supposed to mean? Because we all know that those books that are considered 'non-fiction' might be telling you less of a truth about something than these here 'fiction' books. I'll give you an example: Back when I was in the sixth grade my teacher told me I had to give an oral report about slavery in Africa. Well up until that point I had never heard about this slavery in Africa. So she told me to check out all these 'non-fiction' books about the subject.

Well basically what these 'non-fiction' books told me was that the European people were the baddies and that the African people were the goodies. That the European people had everything to do with putting the African people into boats and shipping them off into slavery and that the African people were the innocents, and had no hand in any of it. Well as it turns out this maybe a lot of baloney you see. Cause when I went to Africa a little while ago, every African that I met, and talked to, told me a slightly different story. Here's what my tour guide Bangnani Dube told me (yes, pronounced just like the joint, 'Doob'):

'No . . . No . . . That 'non-fiction' book that you read in the sixth grade is all wrong . . . all wrong my friend. The Africans had a lot to do with putting their own people into slavery. They really did. You see slavery existed in Africa long before the Europeans came here. Tribes were at war, and at the end of a conflict, it was routine for the defeated to be enslaved. So when the Euros and others got here and saw what was going on they started asking around to see if they could get in on it. The Africans said:

'Okay white man, we'll help you out and do the dirty work for you. We'll go into the hot n' dangerous jungle and rustle up some of our black folk for ya, while you sit here on the coast, tanning your little white ass.'

Cause how would someone know where to look? There was no Google Earth back then. And no signs that said: Slaves over here, hiding behind this wooded hill. Come get'em.

'But listen here white man. Listen. You'd better load us up with lots of booze and lots of guns, and maybe a few of those little white honey bitches to make up for all this trouble you're causing us.'

And so deals were made. And this is what Bangnani Dube and virtually every one of his African brothers told me, and if you don't believe me go to Africa yourself and talk to these guys. Or just stay here and pick up a book of the 'non-fiction' type and start reading it, and begin to believe everything that author tells you, even though most of it isn't true.

Now how all this relates to Pelicula and everything you've read before Valued Reader, I don't know? But here we go getting back to her diary now. Okay?

Dear diary: Today I received a letter that shocked me beyond belief. It was from my mother. And here's what it said:

My dearest Pelicula: I don't know if there's ever a right time to tell anyone a thing like this, but I thought it would be best if you heard it now, so here goes. You see, Pelicula, your father is not your actual father. Yes. It's true. You're not of his stock. You are the child . . . the love child . . . of the very famous French film director and screenwriter Francois Cherbourg. The man is of African descent and author of. . . .

Your story starts many years ago, while I was still living in the village where I grew up. Do you remember the film 'Two Men and a Little Bit of Moonlight' or in French 'Le Clair de Lune Avec Deux Hommes'? Well your mother was an extra on that film and this is where I first met Monsieur Cherbourg. I didn't know for sure at the time. But I know for sure now.

All my love,

Your Mother. . . .

Pelicula put down the letter.
'Is this at all true?' Anna asks.

'I know that she was an extra on the film. I saw the pictures. I remember it being a period piece or something. I think it took place in the early part of the twentieth century.'

'The last one then.'

'Yes.'

'What was the film about?'

'It was a story about a young man, an actor, who leaves the London stage for a chance to go work in Hollywood, much to his parents' chagrin.'

'Huhm. . . .'

'You see the story is very sad because the boy loves his parents. It's not like he was an orphan or anything, or his parents died when he was young and he was raised by an Aunt who diddled him or anything. No. He had a happy childhood, which is rare for someone going into a creative profession (or so they say). His parents were good to him and this is why it makes it doubly difficult for him to do what he does.'

'Is that the film where the lead actor is getting on a boat to America and he's crying himself silly, while everyone is watching him, wondering what the hell is wrong with this guy?'

'Yes. You've seen it?'

'No. But I've caught bits of it on television. Was it a good film?'

'Not really.'

'And what happened when he got to America?'

'Well he gets mugged just as he gets off the boat. The thieves beat the crap out of him and take him for almost everything he has. So there he is stranded in this new country, penniless. . . .'

'Hold on . . . Hold on a second . . . Your mother's just told you that you're the daughter of a famous film director/screenwriter and you're rambling on about some third-rate movie of the week?'

'I know . . . I know. But it can't be helped for some reason.'

'Why not?'

'I don't know?'

And so it was I, Valued Reader, your author, Madeline Macdonald, who eventually came in and told the girls why things were happening so completely out of the ordinary.

'You see ladies, I must apologize. I know it must be frustrating for you to be talking about one thing when you think you ought to be talking about another. But one thing you must always remember, my dear little characters, is that it's not up to you to be deciding what you should be doing or saying. It's up to me. Your author. Now go about your business and forget we've even had this talk.'

And so the girls did what I told them.

'So as I was saying, we've got to track down your mother and see what this is all about.'

'I agree.'

'Great. Let's go.'

'And so the young man from the boat was found dead the next morning thanks to the thieves. But of course that's not what happened in the movie. That's just what happened in the book. This book.'

The girls stop. Start looking around.

'Did you just hear that?'

'Yeah. Yeah. I for sure heard that.'

Ha ha Valued Reader! How did you like that?! That's what you get to do when you write a book! You get to play with your character's heads! Ha ha! Play with your character's heads.

'Pelicula. Now c'mon now, say it.'

'I got a Black Daddy,' she mutters, realizing.

That's right, yeah, you do.

4

So last night I was watching a movie, and in it the lead actress turned to me and said: 'Why don't you get up out of your seat and come n' check things out from up where I am?' And so I did. I walked right up and onto the screen. And you know what? The world that I had known for so long from one place wasn't at all like the world I was seeing now.

5

AN AILING WOMAN

I was once very famous, known virtually everywhere, by everyone. And I've got to tell the truth and say that I have in no way moved on from the memory of all that, of what happened to me then, but I'd sort of kind of like to, at least sometime soon. Oh please let me do that. Let me move on. Sure I'm sure there are some things that you'd like to move on from remembering. I say to you: 'He who recollects a thing he once enjoyed desires again to possess it under the same circumstances as he first enjoyed it.' I didn't write that, but the fellow who did is really long dead, so I don't think he'll mind if I use it. And anyway, he wrote it in Latin, so I'm not really copying him am I?

This isn't going to be a story about how I got here and into this shoddy hospital. (Diagnosed with terminal cancer on my 49th birthday, that's how I got here.) But a story about where I am now going.

Things had begun that day
I had wanted to talk. With some
began a conversation.

'You look troubled my dea
the matter?'

'That you asked me a thing
woman, I am so relieved. So relieved, really I am,
because my life is so totally full of people who care
not one little bit about the way I feel. Not one little
bit. They just care about themselves and that is it.
My problem is this: I've racked up nearly 75,000
dollars in debt. And I know not what to do.'

'And whom is this debt with if I may ask?'

'It is with Visa, MasterCard, and American
Express. And there is some money owing on a loan
and a couple of lines of credit.'

'But how did you get into so much debt, if I
may ask?'

'Through the writing of a book.'

'Through the writing of a book. I see. I see. All
right, so let me ask you this then: Is the debt secured
against anything? Like a car or a house?'

'I have neither and nothing.'

'Okay. Okay. So tell me this: What amount of
credit is still available?'

y that I have about $40,000 still available
ait . . . I think it's closer to $50,000. Yes it is
to $50,000, because American Express just
used my limit the other day.'

'Then your accounts must be in good standing
then.'

'Oh yes. Oh yes they're in very good standing,
I think. Of course they are, if they're still allowing
me credit. Because I make sure to pay off at least the
minimum payment every month.'

'And how do you do that?'

'With the convenience checks that they send
me.'

And then I looked at this young woman and
said,

'You need to write yourself some money then.'

'With what? With the checks?'

'Yes with the checks.'

'And right then and there Valued Reader, I
knew we wuz up to something.'

'It's strange, but I think I just overheard you
talking to someone?'

'What?'

'You just said something to someone about a
Valued Reader?'

'I'm sorry Mam . . . I wasn't talking to anyone. I must have been mumbling to myself . . . people say that I'm a mumbler. I was just looking out the window, and noticing that you have such a beautiful garden out here. It sure looks pretty.'

'Do you want me to help you?'

'I do Mam . . . I do . . . But it's just that. . . .'

'Are you scared?'

'Frankly a little. . . .'

'Don't be. You said that none of this debt was with family, friends or the mafia. Is that correct?'

'Yes. Yes Mam that's correct. I told you who every bit of this debt was with.'

'Then you'll have nothing to worry about if you just do as I say.'

'Yes Mam.'

'All right then now listen to me. Here's what I want you to do. . . .'

'But all this stuff is sort of starting to sound kind of iniquitous, isn't it?'

'What stuff?'

'This stuff you've been telling me.'

'But I haven't told you anything yet.'

'No. No Mam I know you think you haven't, but you have, because you see, I've been writing and rewriting this chapter for quite sometime now and I have a pretty good idea of what it is that you're going to say to me.'

'Say that again?'

'I said that I already have a pretty good idea of what it is that you are going to say to me, because you've said it to me maybe 10 or 15 times already. I can't remember how many times I've gone over and rewritten things.'

'Rewritten what?'

'This book.'

'Oh . . . this book.'

'Yes Mam.'

And I looked at the girl thinking I'd better play along. Oddly, she then said to me,

'Why did you just think that? That I'd better play along. We're characters in a book you know.'

'But of course we are young lady. Of course we are. And ain't it the truth that you're this book's author. So c'mon along now, why don't you tell me what it is that I'm going to say next.'

'No. You're going to tell me.'

'All right then. I will. This debt of yours, I can clear it up.'

'You can, can you?'

'Yes. And once more, even though you've heard this already. . . .'

'But my Valued Reader hasn't.'

'Not only am I going to be able to wipe away your debt clean, totally clean, I might be able to squeeze another 50 grand or so out of old Visa, MasterCard and American Express for ya. Would you like that?'

'I would. And I think my Valued Readers would really appreciate that, too.'

'I don't doubt that they will.'

'I mean, I need money to continue on with this book, don't I?'

'But in order for me to help you, you have to promise me one thing.'

'Name it.'

'That you'll go in for some therapy.'

*

One of the ladies in this place invited me to afternoon tea with her daughter and son. I wanted so badly to enjoy myself. Really I did. But when at the end of the chat the daughter stood up and said to the son:

'You know what Andrew? You should really think about openin up one of these places. These care facility, hospital thingamajiggies.' And the son replied:

39

'That's right Sis. You're right. You're totally right. What with the aging population and everything? Think of all the money we could be making off a place like this.'

I couldn't help but to think what a waste of time my last hour just was.

*

'So Madeline my child max it up! All of it I tell you! Up to your available credit limit of 50 grand. I don't want to see one morsel of credit left on those accounts!'

'And the checks I write to myself? Where do I put them?'

'You need to put them into a savings account at some bank or credit union that has no affiliations whatsoever with any of the institutions that you are in debt with.'

'And why not a checking?'

'Because putting them in a new checking account will force them to do a credit check on you, and you don't want them doing anything like that, do you?'

'Now do I take out all the money at once?'

'Noooo . . . Not all at once. 50 grand is a lot of money. Taking it out all at once might raise a few eyebrows. You have to do it slowly. But not too slowly. 5 grand here. 6 grand there. Know what I mean?'

'Yes Mam.'

'Now where are you going to put the cash once you have it?'

'I can't put it back in another bank?'

'No. Don't be a fool.'

'How about in my apartment then?'

'Where there?'

'Underneath a floorboard?'

'Underneath a floorboard. Yes. Underneath a floorboard is good. But in a fire retardant box, no doubt.'

'What next?'

'You're going to go to the corner of such and such and into a building there. It will be a big building. Tallest one you've ever seen. Get into the elevator and travel all the way up to the top floor. Top floor. A gentleman will be waiting for you. His name will be Mr. Trump. Mr. Donald Trump. One of his former mistresses, well she and I used to know each other. From school, or work, or something like that. She's dead now, but when she was alive we were the best of friends, and if you tell Mr. Trump that I sent you, he'll no doubt start to feel all warm and fuzzy inside and do whatever he can to help you. He will ask you the same questions that I did, and when he finds out that you are 75,000 + 50,000 = 125,000 dollars in debt, and that all of this debt is unsecured and most of it with the major credit card companies, he is going to say this: That you can walk away from this debt of $125,000 dollars in nine months - in just nine months - provided that you do exactly as he says. Which will be:

(a) Sign for him a bunch of legal documents.

(b) Report to him your monthly income for the next nine months.

(c) Take a couple of bullshit credit counseling courses.

And of course:

(d) PAY HIM HIS FEE. Which will be something like 1800 bucks.'

'And this Trump guy? What does he do for a living?'

'He is what's called a Bankruptcy Trustee.'

'A bankruptcy trustee? You mean . . . You mean I'm going into what's called bankruptcy?'

'Yes. Yes you are my dear young lady. Yes you are. And you can thank your lucky stars for that, for it is the single, most beautiful thing that our modern economic system has to offer.'

'Is it? I heard it aint.'

'You will only hear that from those who lose money on such an endeavor. Never from those who make it. Let me remind you that Mr. Trump would be out of a job if it weren't for girls like you.'

'But will I ever be able to borrow again? I mean doesn't my credit rating take a hit?'

'Sure your credit rating will take a hit. But only for a bit. Only for a little bit. For things are never as serious as they seem. And Mr. Trump will let you in on all the ways that you can rebuild your credit very quickly. Very quickly indeed. So quickly in fact that after the nine-month period is over and you've been discharged of all your debts, I guarantee that within a minimum of two years, within a minimum of two years, you'll be up and running and flashing the old credit card again. I guarantee it! In fact I not only guarantee it. I will swear by my soul upon it! Swear by my soul! And within six and sum years, only six and sum, this whole bankruptcy business will be wiped off your credit report altogether! As if it never happened. Isn't it wonderful how it all works?'

'But shouldn't I feel ashamed for having had to do all this?'

'Ashamed? Ashamed at what?'

'All this lying and embezzling.'

'My dear. What is it that we're in right now?'

'A book. We're in a book.'

'That's right. A book. I'm sorry, because for a moment there it felt like we were in one of those warm and fuzzy television commercials put on by your financiers! This is the system baby. This is Capitalism! And a true capitalist knows no morals. He only knows profits. And who better to stick it to than the major financiers of our time?! I want you to think of it like this: You made money off Mr. Visa, Mr. MasterCard and Mrs. American Express. Made money off them so that you can complete your book. Thank not the grant givers, the charity groups, the council this and thats, or whatever other sucky sucky foundations are out there that go into supporting young artists like yourselves. No. Thank not them for nothing. But thank the major financiers of our time. For they are your true benefactors. And why not let the public in on it? Of how you did it. Of how you beat the capitalists at their own game. Once the book is finished of course. You'll be congratulated by everyone for being not only an artist, but a Capitalist one at that.'

'*As easy as one, two, three, back to Madeline and her POV.*'

'The year was 19 something or other, I think Madeline. Silent pictures were on the out and talking pictures were on the in. I was sixteen years old. Sixteen years . . . Hold on wait a minute. Wait a sec young lady. I thought we weren't going to be talking about any of this? My past.'

'What? You don't want to?'

'Well can you at least be honest with your readers and let them know that silent pictures fell out in and around the late 1920's, early 30's. The story I'm about to tell comes many, many years after that. Like 34 years ago ish.'

'Done.'

'I had seen an ad in the local paper inviting girls to come and try out for . . . to audition . . . for a part in a movie. A lead part. I had performed once in my life, playing Lucy in a ninth grade production of 'You're a Good Man Charlie Brown', for four nights, and four nights only, during a chilly and rainy December.'

'Well if you want to go, you'll have to take the bus. . . .'

'My mother said. She was a nurse, you see, at the local hospital, and the car was hers for work. We lived in a small bungalow about 50 miles - or whatever it is in kilometers for those of you who live in every other country except ours - 50 miles from the great big city where the studios are. You know the place. So if I did take the bus it meant changing buses three times, and a trip of almost 2 1/2 hours. A lot of effort, yes, but I had wanted to act from as far back as I can remember. So I made up my mind to do it.'

'How are you for money?'

'My mother asked me.'

'You need some don't you? Here you go then. Here's some bus fare, and some money for lunch, and a little extra in case you get into trouble, which I'd like you to return to me if you don't get into trouble. You know where to find me if you need me. Just ring the hospital. Good luck my dear daughter! Good luck! And remember: That this acting thing is one of the world's oldest professions, it's as old as whoring, and each and everyone of us does it each and every day. Whether we're aware of it or not. Cause life is one big act, one big movie, as I'm sure you've heard me say, before, in some other context or another. You're just going to have to do it in front of an audience, and that takes courage. Why not put yourself in the place of those poor little African children that we see all the time on TV, with their bulging bellies, sad and swollen eyes, sitting there in the dirt, all around them the shit, and the flies buzzing. Think of what life must be like for them and the challenges they face? It'll make your situation seem all too humbling and privileged. So go out there and have fun my dear daughter. Have fun. And just remember it's a ScreenPLAY. Not a screen work. So do just that: Play. Play as if you were a child, and I think you'll be fine.'

CUT TO:

INT. AUTHOR'S APARTMENT - MORNING
MADELINE is seen writing on her computer.

So okay I'll get back to that ailing woman in a sec Valued Reader, but I've just got to tell you something that happened to me in Egypt last week (Yes I used some of my bankruptcy money to take a trip there). I was in a place called the White Desert and I took a day trip with this Bedouin desert tour guide named Badry Hungsobig.

Now I don't know if I've told you this yet Valued Reader, but I'm not a good-looking girl. I'm not. But I thank to god on this day that I wasn't. Cause had I been a little hottie like Pelicula or Anna K, I wouldn't have had a chance with this Hungsobig guy. He would have put his wiener right into me, even if I told him 'Hey, listen buddy, I'm really not that into you.' That wouldn't have stopped him. He was so horny. Talking about sex all the time. It was really starting to annoy me. Here are a few things that he had the nerve to tell me. He was saying:

'Ah Madeline, you know my young friend, you know, I've had sex with more women out here in the desert, in this very desert, than I've had hot dinners at home. This is true. This is totally true. See over there? On top of that rock? That formation there that looks like a mushroom cloud. This fifty-year-old Dutch cougar and I climbed up there once, in the middle of the night, and humped for hours until the sun came up. Humped for hours. We did. I swear. And it was great. Really great! And over there? See over there behind that white rock that looks like a rabbit? I banged two German honey's, doggy style, in broad daylight! Both at the same time. I just couldn't believe my luck, oh my god what fun it was. And that cave over there? See it? I had the good fortune of getting blown in it not once, but twice! Twice by this middle-aged English Woman, who agreed to do it again to me some forty minutes later! Some forty minutes later! Bahhahha! . . . Bahhahha Madeline! . . . Bahhahha!'

He just wouldn't stop. Really offensive stuff that I for sure would've reported him on had I not been traveling in such a male-dominated culture. But I did have a question on my mind that was relatable to all this sex business. So I asked it. I said, 'Badry is it true that all the girls around here get clitoridectomies before their fifteenth birthday?'

'What's that?' he asked me. He didn't know what a clitoridectomy was.

'Well,' I said. 'That's when a woman gets her clitoris clipped off. I've heard that this procedure is done a lot around here.'

'Ah yes,' he said, suddenly realizing what I was talking about. 'This precautionary procedure is done to women around here in the hopes that they don't become at all distracted by sex once motherhood rolls around. We figure that the pleasure of sex, and the pursuit of it, just gets in the way of her being a good mother you see.'

Well I told him that I thought this procedure was most barbaric. Most barbaric indeed.

'Bahhahha my dear young Madeline. Bahhahha! You know you're not the first woman to come to tell me this. No. This is for sure. And I would like to say that I agree with you one hundred percent. One hundred percent. So don't worry. Don't be alarmed. But how about this? I want you to tell me what you think of a male vasectomy. Because I believe it's far worse, far worse, to perform a vasectomy on a man, than it is to perform a clitoridectomy on a woman.'

I was aghast. 'Please tell me how clipping off a woman's clit can even be made to be the least bit less disturbing than giving a man a vasectomy?'

'Because with the one you are interfering with maybe only just pleasure, and with the other you are interfering, for sure, with creativity. And isn't creativity the source of life and maybe even of happiness? But let's stop this chitter chatter for now. For I see that the sun is setting and a woman over there is waving to me so I must go. And you have more important things than me to do anyway. What with that book you're writing,' he said.

DISSOLVE TO:

INT. AUTHOR'S APARTMENT - AFTERNOON
MADELINE is asleep on her bed next to her
computer. Eventually she wakes up, rolls off her
bed, and begins typing.

Okay here we go getting back to that ailing
woman. Sorry but I sometimes never know where
this book is going Valued Reader. Let's be real. I
always never know where this book is going Valued
Reader.

So the ailing woman became famous, lost that
fame, and then lost what no woman in the world
would ever want to lose. Now I hope that what she
told me will be of interest to you. So much so that
you'll want to keep on hearing her story right up
until the end. From the first word to the last. Cuz
that's my job, isn't it? To keep you reading.
Otherwise, fuck man, put this book down. Because I
don't want to be like one of those artists who has to
rely on the public's sympathy for their survival.
Take this guy here for example. This guy I met
yesterday afternoon outside a liquor store. He had

been playing his guitar and singing, and after he finished he said to me:

'Hey there girl. What do you do? What do you do for a living?'

I said, 'Well. I had been working as a nurse's aid at a hospital, but that's not what I wanted to do with my life, so I quit that. Now my days are spent immersed in a book. You could call me a writer, I guess. But I haven't actually published anything yet.'

He was aflutter. 'A writer? You're a writer? Well then my little artistic sister, what are you waiting for? Throw some cash into this here old guitar case and help me out. I'm really struggling right now, you see. My old lady left me and took my son. Alimony all the time baby. Alimony all the time.'

And here is why Valued Reader that there was no way in the world I was going to give this guy a cent:

'Because my friend you played so badly. Real, real badly. And I wasn't at all entertained. So for me to subsidize any of that shit is unthinkable. Totally unthinkable. Play better and I'll float you some money. Otherwise get a real job.'

Now all I'm saying Valued Reader is that I just don't want you to be reading this book because you think you have to. I want you to be reading this book because you really want to. What do you think this is? School or something?

'So from the time I'd gotten that part Madeline, the one I'd auditioned for when I was 16, to the time I was 24, I'd become a working actress. Known everywhere around the globe, except for in those places that didn't have the technology yet to comprehend what a movie star was. Kidding. I was nowhere near that famous, like I'd said earlier. But if I'd said yes to Uber Girl I would've been. Would've been for sure . . . So on the night when it all happened, when everything began to change, I remember being so fully loaded with this anxiety that I still hadn't bothered to learn the 7 3/8 pages worth of dialogue that I needed for my scene tomorrow.'

Yipee! Hooray! Time to light up that fatty. Cause guess who's just arrived? None other than BLACK DADDY!

'Pelicula? Pelicula are you awake?'
'Yes Black Daddy. What is it?'

'I just dreamt of that actress again.'

'You mean the blonde gal from the other night?'

'Yes and oh my god, she was even more beautiful in this dream than in the one before. And you know what? This is not a lie. I thought of doing things to her that only you and I can talk about.'

So on the night when it all began to change for our young heroine Katherine Whitaker (aka, the ailing woman):

'It must have been 1900hrs that evening when I got home. I had exercised, showered, changed, made some dinner, eaten, and dranken a bit, but decidedly not too much, because like I said, I still had a lot of work to do for tomorrow's scenes.'

'Mmmmmmm . . . Well if you're going to get with a lady like that my Black Daddy Genius, and I know you want to, you're going to have to give her something more than what an ordinary man can give. It's only right.'

'Write something for her then.'

'Yes. That's what you should do.'

'And leave it there. In the HOUSE. In MY HOUSE. For her to find . . . oh dear god, Pelicula! That's what I'll do!'

QUICK CUT TO:

INT. AUTHOR'S APARTMENT - EVENING
Madeline is sobbing, very violently, next to her computer. Hold on this for a bit until we eventually start to:

FADE OUT AND INTO THE NEXT CHAPTER:

6

Valued Reader. Please excuse me. I'm sorry. There needs to be an explanation here. Something's just happened. A girl, a young lady, whom you'll meet very soon, just broke into Madeline's apartment and stole her book. Burned it to a 16g memory stick, and then went ahead and deleted every saved copy that Madeline had. This is hot stuff. Really hot stuff. So stay tuned. . . .

7

DISSOLVE TO:

INT. NEW AUTHOR'S APARTMENT - DAY
A YOUNG WOMAN, mid-twenties, is seen writing on her laptop. Her place is better decorated than Madeline's was. Roughly the same size though.

A handsome man whom I liked very much once said to me that if I'm on my way somewhere, and in a hurry, and have a hold on a bag that is just way too heavy for me then 'why don't I just move forward without it?' That is, why not be looking for a place to store it? For the time being anyway. I could always come back for it later. You know I left you once Valued Reader and I'm a little upset with myself for having done that. But a girl has got to do what she's got to do. Let me make it up to you by saying that I'm sorry for taking off, and that I missed you. There that's done. I said it. Now let's move on. Madeline couldn't tell the ailing woman's story. She couldn't. I'm sorry. Using her own voice.

It simply didn't work. And I tried writing it that way countless times. I really did. But there was lacking in Madeline's delivery some sort of, I don't know, undeserved quality that the story of Katherine Whitaker needed to be told with. That was her name you know, Katherine Whitaker. At least that was her real name. Madeline and I never knew what her screen name was. Even though we asked her, oh I don't know, how many times. I had Katherine do it. Because she did such a stellar job of telling you guys how to go about shafting Visa, MasterCard and American Express for all that money. Talk about yourself then Katherine please. You have my permission. But she couldn't. And I don't know why, but I think it may have had something to do with the opinion you already hold of her. So that being said I am now going to tell you in my own words the story of Katherine Whitakers. Sorry Whitaker. And I'm also going to let you in on a secret: Madeline Macdonald is no longer writing this book anymore Valued Reader. It's me, Ms. Abigail Adams, her former hospital co-worker, former roommate, and former something else, who'll be doing it. Now I hope I haven't steered your attention away from Katherine by telling you all this. I really hope I haven't.

Katherine had said that what'd happened to her at the start of her career had a lot to do with luck.

'I was a great match for the woman who played my mother. Simple as that. Same hair color, eyes, skin tone. Both Caucasian.'

The studio had initially offered the part of her mother to two other 'name' actresses already, who didn't look at all like Katherine.

'If either of those two ladies had said yes then I'd have still been delivering newspapers around the time I was signing autographs. This is true. Totally true.'

She was good at giving herself credit though.

'At least I did it. Didn't I? Which is more than a lot of people can say for themselves. There's merit in that. Listen I could've gone and done what my friends were doing at the time. Getting it on with boys, boozing it up, experimenting with drugs. But I didn't. I got up at six every morning and took the bus for 2 1/2 hours every other day for a month and went and sweated it out at those grueling, awful auditions. And what for? For a shot at doing something I loved. I had wanted to play, and if you want to play you have to get in the game. Take a chance. It's like fishing. Put your line in the water. The fish won't jump in the boat.'

This wasn't smack she was talking. If it weren't for her I don't know what I would've done. I wouldn't have called off my wedding probably.

By the end of her life Katherine never wondered 'why' it'd all happened.

'Life must simply unfold the way that it does. Why do you want to go making sense of Providence? Only the fools and egomaniacs always want to do that. Providence need not have to explain itself to you. To you, this piddly little human, with your finite little mind. Go to the artist if you want someone to wipe your nose for you. To give you an explanation of things. That's their job. They should be doing that. I'm just grateful to have been born what I was anyhow. A human-body-mind organism. It would have sucked to have been born otherwise. Like to have been born a goat.'

What did Katherine look like around the time she was twenty-four? I don't know. But I do know that her hair had once been blonde. A beautiful blonde. Just like Pelicula's.

'I can thank my mother, my grandmother, my great-grandmother, my great-great-grandmother, and my great-great-great-grandmother for that. They were of Dutch descent.'

This must have been where she got her eyes too. They were a most magnificent, mysterious color. If ever you go to see the Taj Mahal in the morning and then go back later in the day to look at it, you'll notice that it's a different color. Made so by the difference in light. Well this was what it was like looking into Katherine's eyes. You were never sure what color they were. Were they hazel? Are they blue? Are they green? She had amazing skin.

'And this was because of the blender drinks I had every morning. I made them myself. Never anyone else. Fresh kale, beats, ginger, turmeric, carrots, broccoli, and hemp hearts.'

'Hemp hearts?' I said.

'Yes, Abigail, hemp hearts. Only movie stars had them back then. They weren't available to civilians.'

She never smoked. And was a sensible drinker. She was beautiful after all. Beautiful. A goddess incarnate.

'And as far as my body went Abigail, well it was one of those bodies that men lusted over. A real baby making body. It was a body steeped in fertility, and if you have one of those Abigail well you can really turn a man on. Really grab his attention and make him get a boner.'

'And what is it that attracts a woman?'

'Getting a woman's attention isn't as simple, Abigail. It isn't. Women are much more complex than men. Conception is ours by nature, you know. But really, I'm sure it's much the same thing. It has something to do with creativity. Just ask any artist, athlete or anyone who invents or makes something. I bet they get laid a lot if they want.'

She said she'd been shooting for over a month already.

'Yes Abigail. Yes. And I was on the East Coast. The East Coast of this grand, imperial country, that's where I was at. Near Charleston, South Carolina. And staying in a house that overlooked the water. The view of the sea was amazing. Absolutely amazing. I would go out there every morning and watch the sun as it would come up, and then head out there later in the evening and watch it as it came down. It humbled me to look at it.'

The house itself wasn't all that extravagant, she said.

'No, Abigail, it wasn't a fancy-ass, frilly place. No it wasn't. It was a simple one bedroom and den, single-level dwelling. Maybe totaled 1200 square feet. It was perfect for one person. Absolutely perfect . . . Unless of course you were born a poor third worlder, where it would've been not only perfect for you, but for your entire impoverished village as well. . . .'

The furniture she said was a blend of classic and modern.

'That's right. It was a little bit of both. The bed in the bedroom was of French colonial design. Made of solid brass and full of lots of nicks and scrapes that told you all sorts of things about it.'

And she said that everywhere in the living room there was the smell of fresh leather.

'I had the chair and sofa to thank for that. They were new. So going in there was like heading into the showroom at Pottery Barn. You know that smell, don't you? You either love it or hate it. Well I loved it.'

The light fixtures were all new too, she said, but designed with antiquity in mind.

'But the dining room table was old, Abigail. Genuinely old. As if 4 or 5 generations of subjects had already eaten their breakfast, lunch and supper off of it. It was made I think in 17 something or other. Around the time of the Declaration of Independence. Yes. Around that time. Hardwood floors everywhere, which I loved. Except in the bathroom I think. No wait a minute I think they were in the bathroom too. All in all I'd have to say that the place had a very masculine bravura to it which I liked. And you know, I didn't know who lived there. At least not right away I didn't.' (And this is important for you to remember Valued Reader. So remember this okay.) 'You would have thought, Abigail, that there would've been some pictures on the walls, or something lying around, some mail coming in, phone calls, or this or that, diploma, awards, anything that would've given away an identity. But there wasn't. There was nothing. And no one from the film knew anything either. Not the producer. Not the production manager who had rented it for me. All they knew was that I was content. And for a short time, anyways, I was.'

She'd been learning her lines. That's what she'd been doing on that portentous night so long ago.

'I was maybe 15 percent off-book. And that's a big maybe. It was like 9 in the evening and I had to be up in the morning, early. So I had a plan: I would work my ass off until around 1. Get to bed after that, because after all I needed some sleep. Set the alarm for 6 and be out the door by 615. At work by 630.'

It was a game plan that sounded all wrong to me. So all wrong. She was a woman after all.

'Uhm Katherine, didn't you need time to get ready in the morning. Like most women do?'

'But remember Abigail, I wasn't a normal woman. I was a movie actress. All that morning stuff, like the hair, the makeup, the nails, picking out of our clothes, pressing them, I didn't have to do any of that. It was all done for me once I got there. For me, getting up in the morning was pretty much like being a man. I just got up and went.'

Never on a night before a big scene like this had she been so underprepared. Never.

'No Abigail, you're right. Never. I was always very disciplined. Right from the get go. Talent only gets you so far. You must know that.'

So why was she in this mess? How come this was happening to her?

'I'll say it was a force to be reckoned with. That's what I'll say it was . . . Or a force to be accepted. Maybe that's a better way to put it.'

I asked her if maybe this whole force to be accepted thing was just a bunch of baloney and that maybe it was simple fear that had put her in this spot. She just went 'whatev. . . .' and gave a wave of her hand.

'Holy wow and holy cow there is the truth of it all right there. In a nutshell. Said to me by my very own Little Miss Nursy Aid. That my career as an actress, as one of the biggest movie stars on the planet, ended because of fear. Fear of what? Of going on?'

She paused for a second and gave this some thought, but eventually shook her head.

'No. No. The truth won't cut it in this case I'm afraid. Too boring. Better to make something up off the top of my head. That will serve us much better. Remember now Abigail: It isn't important that a story be true. But it is after all important that it be compelling. You of all people should know that.'

'Now Abigail learning lines is hard work. After awhile your mind just goes nowhere and everywhere and you can't seem to think straight about anything.'

At around 10pm she . . . 'decided to take a break. I went into the kitchen and poured myself a glass of wine. Looking up I saw . . . WTF? . . . a light in the den had come on?! How had that happened? It had been days since I'd last been in there. Maybe weeks. Now I wasn't scared, thinking that maybe someone had broken into the place. These were the good old days remember? People just didn't do that sort of thing. The times were much 'simpler' then. Oh nostalgia. Sweet nostalgia. Helping us phony up the world since I don't know when.'

'Now Abigail never believe the fools and the ignoramuses who tell you that you are the one in control. Control is an illusion. Simple as that. And if you don't believe me then try holding your bowels for an entire week and see what sort of control you have over something like that. We are slaves to nature first. Then to the ineffable after. Which is what I was up against on that night.'

Her answer was forthcoming when I asked her why it was that she never went into the den.

'Why? Well it wasn't cause I didn't like it. No that wasn't it. Problem was that there was no natural light in there. Nada. And I just adore natural light. Just adore it. And here's the thing. There could've been a ton of natural light in there. A ton. If it hadn't of been for the owner, who'd taken this one big giant slab of cardboard and pasted it all over the one giant window. I mean nuts! And what a view of the sea you would've had from there too. Aaaaamazing. Absolutely amazing.' (You'll know soon enough why the cardboard was on the window Valued Reader. Don't worry.)

I asked her what else was in there.

'On the walls? On the walls there was only one thing: A map of the world with tiny inkblots all over it. On all sorts of towns, cities and places. Blots in the Americas. In Africa. In Asia. There were even blots in the Antarctica. Or very close to Antarctica anyway. A desk. A typewriter. Some foolscap paper. And just north of the paper were these pencils. 15 of them. In rows of 3 by 5. Sharpened and ready to go. Umm, what else? A desk chair and a very large sofa chair.'

'Could you have slept in the chair?' I asked.

'Yes Abigail. Yes. You could have slept in the sofa chair. But here we are getting ahead of ourselves, aren't we?'

(Foreshadowing   Valued   Reader. Foreshadowing.)

'But, Abigail, the piece of furniture in the den that intrigued me the most was the Indian Armoire. It was made right around the time of the early Raj, in a city that used to be called Bombay, but that is now called Mumbai.'

'You looked inside this Armoire, I take it? To see what was in there.'

'Oh, Abigail, I tried opening the Armoire the day I arrived, but I found out it was locked, and I couldn't find a key anywhere in the house. And I looked everywhere for one. Really I did.'

I was appalled. Told her that she was a snoop.

'A snoop? Oh, Abigail, I am a snoop. I'm a big snoop. Whatev, whoop, dee do. Snoopy do . . . So okay, c'mon, tell me . . . What is it that you have against snooping? Is it that you're terrified of being caught? Or terrified at what you might find?'

So that light in the den? How had it come on?

'Oh, for the sake of appealing to the masses Abigail, let's just say that that light in the den had ALWAYS been on. Ever since I'd arrived in that house it had been on. Never had I noticed it before. That is all.'

She was seeing the light for the very first time. Very interesting Valued Reader. Very interesting.

'I mean c'mon, really? Did I want to go back to where my script was? In the kitchen.'

Her script Valued Reader. Her script.

'I wanted to stay in the den, where I was, with the Armoire. The Armoire. The large and beautiful. . . .' *But wait a minute Katherine. It's 1024pm. You have to get back. Back to learning your lines.* 'And there they were Abigail. There they were . . . the italics from my diary. Never failing to materialize whenever I was under duress. . . .'

So there she was, standing underneath the den door threshold, ready to turn off the light.

'When, Abigail, suddenly it dawned on me. I needed something that was in there. Needed it more than anything. But I became frightened, said to myself quit it, and turned the light down anyway. But Abigail I wasn't moving. In the darkness there I was, standing motionless. Then, suddenly, to my amazement, everything in the den became illuminated once again. The desk, the two chairs, the paper, the pencils, the typewriter, the map of the world, the cardboarded window, the Armoire . . . the lovely and beautiful . . . But WTF? I hadn't touched the switch. Miraculously, on its own, with no interference whatsoever on my part, it came back up.'

But you know what you're supposed to be doing Katherine. So why aren't you doing it?

'Oh, I know diary italics, I know.'

So she tried turning down the light a second time, but the same thing happened, the light came back up.

'I was starting to think that maybe someone was trying to tell me something.'

Nevertheless she persisted, turning down the light a third time.

'But to no avail, Abigail. To no avail.'

Then a fourth time. Then a fifth. A sixth. A seventh.

'And each time it went down, it kept coming up again. I was flabbergasted.'

An eighth time she tried. A ninth. A tenth. An eleventh. A twelfth. A thirteenth. A fourteenth. A fifteenth. A sixteenth. A seventeenth. An eighteenth. A nineteenth. Until finally on the twentieth try, she just blurted out:

'Oh for fuck's sake Katherine. If the light in the den must be on, then why not leave it on? Say it is so and see how it plays out.'

And with this in mind, wild, mirthful laughter began spilling from her.

'Right then and there in the middle of the den, Abigail, I just exploded. And it felt so good to be doing that. So good to be laughing. Now tell me? What other animal on this planet gets to laugh, and laugh like us? Umm? Tell me? You want to say the hyena. I know you do. But please don't mention that thing. Please don't.'

What's that you say you just saw Katherine? A ghost?

'Yeah, but I don't believe in ghosts.'

But you say you just saw one?

'I know. But I still don't believe in them. A classic case for denial I am, I know. But alone here I'm not. Very few people are into having their belief systems challenged. You know this to be true. And so do I.'

What were to follow were even more surprises.

'All that hocus-pocus stuff? It wasn't finished with me yet, cause look. Right there in the lock of the Armoire, there was a KEY. That's right a key. A big shiny, brass key, and on the base of it were those masks.'

'Masks?' I asked.

'Yes, those masks, Abigail. You know the ones. You used to see them all the time hanging outside live theatre venues, back when live theatres were still in existence. One mask is of a HAPPY face. The other is of a SAD face. They represent the twin themes of joy and despair. Of the comedy of life. Of the tragedy of it. The masks used to be worn in resistance to conformity. Back in the day. Put one on and, there you go, you can now express your true self, without any fear.'

'Hiding behind a mask to express one's true self. I like that. Like that a lot.'

'Yes I know, Abigail. Knew you would. But listen, all this talk about folklore? Is it really getting us anywhere?'

The time Katherine. Look at the time.

'All I wanted was one quick peek. That's it, and that's all. Oh, I 'love how we always say that. One quick this. One quick that. One quick bite of the cake. Well lookie here, it's all gone. One quick drink. Yes, bye, bye bottle. A quick kiss? Huh, whatta ya know, I'm pregnant. But for its amusements, life would be tolerable. I didn't come up with that, but let us all agree with the man who did.'

Slowly, very slowly she put her wine glass down.

'Next to the typewriter on the desk.'

It's 1040 Katherine, your lines, you have to get back to learning your lines.

And then she heard it. And heard it clearly.

'Heard what? Oh, yes that click. That click that tells you that the lock has been picked.'

So she inched back a little and took hold of the handles.

'With my hands, Abigail. Tell whomever you're talking to that I grabbed the handles with my hands.'

Music started to play. It was from the first movie she'd ever been in.

'So sweet.'

A gust of wind swept in.

'A very, very powerful gust of wind. From who knows where. It started messing up my clothes. My hair.'

It had force equal to that of a tornado.

'But a force equal to that of a phony movie tornado you mean.'

The floor started rumbling. The lights began shaking. Her wine glass tipped over.

'Blasphemy. No it didn't.'

The desk, the pencils, the paper, the two chairs, the typewriter, the map of the world, the cardboarded window, the Armoire. The lovely and beautiful . . . Oh c'mon Katherine. C'mon now tell us. What was in there? What was in that Armoire?

'All right I will tell you. Abigail there were BOOKS in there. Lots and lots of books. This large and beautiful Armoire was nothing and everything but a library.'

I was right away not impressed and told her so. 'Oh man, books? Holy moly, that's dull. Why not instead pull a shenanigan from one of your films?

Put in there, say, a magic portal to some far-off land.'

But there was no amusing her with this. Suddenly she became very serious.

'There were books in there, Abigail. Books and nothing else.' (Valued Reader there was definitely something else in there. Definitely something else in there.) 'Books by guys and gals who I'm sure you've all heard about, but never read. Or if you have read them, you read them in school, which is really not like reading anything at all. Classic books. All dead writers. Anywhere dead from 75 years to 2000 years. Now listen, you want a fucking portal to some far-off land? Well you're not going to get it. At least not from me you're not. Cause that fucking portal that you see up there on the screen leads to this: It leads to the other end of the MOVIE SOUND STAGE. Which leads to a bathroom, where you take a shit. I'm so fed up with all this supernatural movie bunk bullshit that's been happening to me tonight. So fed up with it. I mean whataya trying to do? Disillusion me?'

'So should we move out of here, and away from all this?'

'Yes but first let me say this: That it was on this night, that night of all nights, that I was first hit with the inspiration to do what you're doing Abigail. To write.'

'That's so cool. Now Katherine listen, listen. I'm going to be absent from work for the next couple of months. For at least the next couple of months.'

'Young lady. To where are you going?'

'To West Africa. Cape Coast Castle to be exact. In and around where they used to house the slaves. I'll be volunteering there to help the poor and implement organic farming. . . .'

And at the mention of this Valued Reader, Katherine fainted. Next, all I remember was there was a doctor rushing in.

8

And with each book she picked up, falling from it was a note of foreign currency. 'From a country here. A country there. China, Brazil, Peru, India, Russia and many, many more. I was looking, thinking, now had this person actually been to all these places or had they just sent away for these things, like nerds do stamps?'

9

But she changed her mind anyway and wanted to move forward in a movie direction after all. 'Oh all righty then, all right. Ramp it up. Ramp up the old movie magic bullshit for one last go around. If not for old times' sake. But what da ya say we go and see what it looks like behind the screen after this?' 'Done, done, and done,' I told her.

10

Now I hope you don't mind Valued Reader if we dispense with your current author for a bit, or perhaps for ever. This next part has to be written by someone who knows a thing or two about the movie biz, and Abigail doesn't unfortunately.

11

This, a recent VIDEO CALL, between two friends.

'Hold it up. Let me see it. What'd ya have there?'

'It's some sort of novel, slash, screenplay, slash, whatever or other, film treatment, I guess.'

'You found it?'

'Found it underneath a floorboard in this low budget backpacker hotel room. In Africa. It was just sitting there. Inside a fire retardant box, next to like 505 bucks cash. It's so hard to say what it's about. So much indecipherable chicken scratch, shit handwriting.'

'Is there a movie in it?'

'Yeah. Maybe. Just maybe.'

12

Now Valued Reader this Man you see before you he is what's called a Stand-in. Arguably the dullest job on a film set.

13

INT. MOVIE SOUND STAGE - MORNING
A MAN, mid-20's, sits in the corner of the stage, alone, writing on his computer.

Okay fuck man here we go. Good movie. Good movie. We are interior den. Morning. Morning calm after the storm. Let's say we start with a CLOSE-UP (CU) of Katherine's face. She is asleep. A few beats ensue, stay on this, then: DISSOLVE INTO Katherine's dream. In this dream she is giving birth. Holy jumpin Toledo, Ohio. Giving birth. Now there's no one else around in this dream. No doctor. No nurse. No male baby maker. She's all on her own. Okay Katherine you must wake up now. Wake up.

WE PULL BACK and reveal our heroine slouched in the armchair, the big cushy armchair, next to the Armoire. Lifting her head, she says to herself,

'The den. I'm in the den.'

And that's right ladies and gentlemen. Katherine slept in there. In the den. There's the Armoire to her left. The Armoire. So suddenly, so magically it opened up last night, dispelling Katherine's curiosity.

'There were lots of books in there. Lots and lots of books,'

And what else? What else? Oh, Katherine, dear Katherine. You're trying to remember what else it was that you found in there, aren't you?

And maybe for a split second she does, remember, but . . . QUICKLY PAN the camera over. We watch, watch, as her gaze falls to the clock on the wall. Wam! Bam! Thank you Mam! ZOOM IN. The clock says 730am. Holy shit. Like a jack rabbit she jumps up, rushes the hell out of there, straight into the shower. That's right Katherine. You're late. Late for work.

Now eliminate all the shit of her getting out of the shower, putting on a t-shirt and yoga pants, just CUT TO:

Zoom, zoom, zoom. WIDE ANGLE. Katherine's car speeds down the highway. Then CUT TO: INSIDE THE STUDIO LOT DAY. That fast? So soon? Yes so soon. Let's get to this. This is a movie after all. Not a novel. Quit pissing around.

Fuck all the flowery language bullshit. On the studio lot we see the actor's trailers. Producer's trailer. Director's trailer. Hair and makeup trailer. Grip trucks. Electric trucks. Camera trucks. Wardrobe trucks. Catering truck. Catering tent. Background holding tent. Am I missing anything? All these things abound. It's like a circus. A modern-day circus has come to town. And which town is this? Some town on the East Coast. The East Coast? Right, it could be the West Coast, but let's just not let the audience in on this. Why? I don't know why. Just let's not.

BIG WIDE as we watch Katherine's car pull up onto the lot. CRANE DOWN. Katherine, exits her car. Rushes towards her trailer in a frantic sort of way. She steps up, opens the door, disappears inside, and as she does this FRAME UP on a tired, gaunt-looking man in his late twenties standing nearby. PUNCH IN. Punch in on him. This man is the 3rd Assistant Director. 3rd AD. Spotting Katherine, he radios ahead to his superiors. And who are his superiors? Here,

CUT TO: INSIDE OF THE STUDIO. MORNING. The 1st Assistant Director is receiving word that Katherine has arrived.

'Copy that.'

He then walks on over to a FIT-LOOKING MAN in his early 50's. Reports the news,

'Katherine's arrived.'

The fit-looking man nods his head. Meet Zack the director of this, our, MOW. MOW? What does that mean? (M)ovie (O)f the (W)eek. Movie for television. Get it? The movie is set in England. Period piece. Early 1900's to be sort of exact. Based on a series of moderately selling books. The title? Through The Glass Television. That's the title? Yes, but everyone says it's too long so they want to change it.

'But if we change it how will our audience know it's from the books?'

'Who gives a shit? You just change it.'

Here's the story. It's basically absurd. There's these two twentysomething girls named Maddy and Abby. They're roommates. Well maybe they're 'more than just roommates'. Maybe, just maybe. The girls need a new television. Da. So they go to a garage sale to look for one. Score. They find one on the cheap and take it home. Plug it in, turn it on. That evening Maddy . . . Maddy? Is it Maddy? Yes, Maddy is loitering close to the television and well what da ya know? Holy fuck her hand goes right through?! Right fucking through! She calls her bestie over. 'Abby look!' The girls can't believe it. Like holy fuck. They bought a magic television. Both of them are thinking WTF? Guess what happens next? Guess? Maddy takes it one step further. Sticks her entire head into the TV. When she pulls her head back out she says to Abby, 'Baby I'm going in.' Course Abby just has to follow her. Just has to. Now here's the gag. When you jump through the magic television, YOU don't become YOU on the other side. YOU become whatever, whomever, whatever it was on the screen, most in focus, center of frame, when you made the jump. Jump while Joan of Arc is on the screen and you become Joan of Arc in 1427 or whenever the hell Joan was rockin it. Jump when some little peasant extra is featured on the screen, you get to become that little peasant extra. Jump when there's a close-up of a bullfrog, well YOU become that bullfrog. Now what characters did the girls become on their first adventure? Well none other than two of the most favored, most sought after, most requested concubines of the late Ashanti King, King Kusi Obodum, ruler of what would now be present day Ghana. Quite a turn of events for these young ladies, I know. . . .

Now to get back. The return. Here's the trick. There has to be someone or some force to turn the television off from where it was that you made the jump otherwise you're hooped. Hooped. You're stuck being that person, slash thing, that was on the screen when you took off. Now fortunately, very fortunately, for Maddy and Abby, on their first jump, their cleaning lady was around to help them out. 'My, my, my. Don't those blasted little princesses know how to waste energy!' she was grumbling, after having spotted that the television was on and no one was home. Wam! Bam! Thank you cleaning lady mam! Television gets turned off and Maddy and Abby return home safely. Now no one is ever able to fully remember their magic television journey. No, no, no. This is part of the gag. But Maddy and Abby did confess that the experience of being King Kusi's favorite ladies had made them want to be 'more' than friends, even just a little more.

Quick CUT TO KATHERINE in her TRAILER, rather frantically putting on her PERIOD PIECE WARDROBE.

Oh and one more thing about the MOW we're doing. Forget everything I just told you. We're not telling that story now. Things have changed. You see a Christian network put up the money for this thing and several of the bigwig executives started to get cold feet when they heard that Maddy and Abby were probably more than just friends. 'What will our advertisers think? All this potential lezzie shit?' So no longer are there two girls anymore doing the jumping. There's just one. And her name is Mabby. And this is who Katherine is playing.

KATHERINE in her TRAILER putting on her period piece wardrobe. Flash on the screen: Playing Mabby in this MOW.

Now in this scene that's coming up, the one we're getting ready to shoot, Katherine/Mabby jumped through the television, and landed in 1917. The scene is this, it's early morning, and Katherine/Mabby has just come in from a night of hanging out with theatre types. Vagabond reprobates. At least this is what her mother calls them. Doesn't like her daughter hanging out with this crowd. Wants her precious daughter to marry this rich boy named Johnnie. That way she'll be all set up. Safe and secure, with cash. But her daughter doesn't want to do any of this. 'I have other plans mother.' The girl wants to board a ship that's heading to America. Then once there, 'I'll join a vaudevillian theatre group.' 'And after that?' Her mother asks. 'Then it's off to California. Where a new art form has begun to revolutionize the world

and I want to be part of it: MOTION PICTURES.'
Her mother can't think straight. Almost falls over.
'Oh, what is it that you're doing with your life,
young lady? What is it that you're doing?'

Now I'm sure you've heard this story before,
or at least one similar to it. So sure you have.

So back to KATHERINE in her trailer
frantically putting on her 1917 wardrobe. Stay on
this for a sec. Only for a sec, then maybe dissolve to
where I am on the sound stage. Wait a minute? To
where you are? What the fuck you talking about
boy?

FADE OUT AND
INTO THE NEXT
CHAPTER:

14

DISSOLVE TO:

INT. MOVIE SOUND STAGE - MOMENTS LATER
As before, this guy is typing away on his computer in the corner of the sound stage.

Like why not? Why not put yourself in a movie? So there. Here I am in this movie. So what happens next? Zack the fit-looking director comes over, starts talking to me. Asks me about the script I'm writing.

'Can you tell me about it?'

'Sure. Sure I can. It's based, partially, on an unfinished manuscript I found in Ghana, West Africa and on a reality that has yet to play out here.'

'Two realities yet unrealized. I like that. Like that a lot.'

And just like that we were off.

Okay so DISSOLVE TO KATHERINE stepping out of makeup and hair. She is now ready. Fully dressed. Fully made-up. She looks great. All periodED up. 1917ished up. Starts walking to set. Gets to set. Right away, rushes over to you, sir. Says,

'I'm sorry Zack, for being late.' You say,

'Nonsense dear. Nonsense. We just went ahead and did some insert shots. Of hands playing the piano or something like that. So no time was wasted sweetie. No worries, you didn't hold things up.' Now this is called lying, but if it helps to make a woman feel better, well why not? Happy wife, happy life. Right? Go ahead tell that woman she looks good, when she really doesn't. Go ahead tell that woman she's lost weight, when she really hasn't. Go ahead tell that woman that she doesn't need makeup, when she undoubtedly does. Look at how all this lying has worked on Katherine. She looks relieved, so relieved that she didn't hold things up. Says to you,

'Oh, I'm so sorry Zack I don't know what got over me. I just fell asleep in the den. There was no alarm in there.' Her mind starts drifting to the den . . . to the Armoire. She starts thinking . . . What else was in the Armoire other than books?

Look man she doesn't want to disappoint you. You're like a father figure to her. You got her started in this business after all. Gave her that lead in a movie. Eight years ago. She was sixteen. Thousands upon thousands of other starry-eyed teenagers auditioned for her part. But you gave it to her, sir. Dam. She must owe a lot to you. Or does she? Da, da, da dum . . . The plot thickens. See bottom line sir is Katherine is starting to change. She's starting to not believe in what she's doing. Oh I know, you say, we're all kind of a little bored with this cheesy little Movie of the Week crap. But wait Katherine . . . Wait until you hear the news.

'Wait a minute, what news?'

'It's career altering. Come see me in my office at lunch, sweetie. Come see me in my office at lunch.'

Well let's get to it then. Let's say it's lunch already. Wow that morning went fast. Well hold on. This morning's work. What did we do? This, we did one big wide master shot. How many takes? One take. Two takes. That's all we needed. Then we went in for coverage. Actress playing KATHERINE'S MOTHER. Her coverage. This woman, so scared, so jealous, of what her daughter is doing. Children. All they do is upset their parents. All right enough yackadee yack.

'Picture's up. C'mon let's shoot.'

'Roll camera.'

'Camera rolling.'

'All right action.'

C'mon mother act. Act, act, act. One take, two takes, three takes.

'Awesome!'

'Brilliant!'

'Going tighter.'

'Swapping a lens.'

'75 millimeter?'

'No maybe 100 millimeter lens.'

'All right picture's up. Ring the bell. Sound speed.'

'Sound is speeding.'

1 take. 2 takes. 3 takes. 4 takes.

'Nice work. Okay we're done. Done with the mother.'

'That's lunch. 1 hr lunch.'

'Copy that.'

'We'll turn around on Katherine after lunch.'

'Turn the camera around on Katherine after lunch.'

At catering sir, here we are. The crew is queuing up. Food on an American film set? Is it really what it's cracked up to be? Civilians want to know. Today's menu is, you have a choice of grilled chicken, lamb skewers, or this veggie three-bean pilaf dish. Choice? What do you mean choice? This is film. Go have all three if you want. You're allowed. Soups. Two of them. Dairy-free pumpkin or French onion. Starches. Baked yams, or garlic mashed potatoes. Vegetables. Steamed broccoli, honey-glazed carrots, or this baked eggplant and onion dish covered with mozzarella cheese. Salads. There's three different types. There's a caesar salad with gluten-free croutons. There's a kale and avocado salad, sprinkled with Parmesan cheese. Or a vinaigrette beet salad mixed with shredded cucumber. And for dessert? Why there's chocolate cake, crème brûlée or fresh fruit. And guess what civilians? Guess? It's absolutely free. Free with the days work. Now beat that.

Okay sir so there you are in your office. You hear a knock. At the door. You look up. It's Katherine.

'Come in, come in,' you say to her. She sits down. In front of your desk. 'How did you like the bean dish?'

'The bean dish?' She's wondering what the hell you're talking about? She obviously didn't have some.

'Awww Katherine, c'mon, didn't you have some of the bean dish? It was amazing, absolutely amazing.'

She says, 'Maybe next time.' Doesn't really want to talk about food. Wants to know why you brought her here? Kind of unusual, is it not?

All right let's get to it, then. Let's quit fucking around and tell her the news. One of the major studios is moving forward with a big-budget screen adaptation of Uber Girl and . . . She suddenly interrupts you.

'Uber Girl? Who is this Uber Girl?' She tells you she's never heard of Uber Girl before.

'Ah, c'mon Katherine, what? You been living under a rock? Fucking Uber Girl.'

'Oh, wait a minute,' she says. 'Wait a minute.' She has heard of Uber Girl before. Yes. She tells you,

'I was over at my best friend Anna Kipolski's parent's place for dinner, not too long ago. Anna's little brother, this pimply-faced, obnoxious little wanker, was stuck in front of the television playing a video game. He wouldn't come to eat. He was telling his mom, mom leave me alone, I'm not hungry. What video game was he playing? That little pimply-faced wanker was playing Uber Girl.'

Okay, so, quick cut to Uber Girl's hashtag bio:

#Mid twenties #Hottie #Blondie #Ass kicking #Good tits #Good booty #But not too big booty #This is America after all #Superheroine suit that exposes her midriff #Into archeological shit #From an aristocratic family #Parents are? #Dead #Of course they are #Killed by the Egyptian terrorist Badry Hungsobig #Uber Girl's arch nemesis #She's got to stop him #Fucking stop him #Otherwise he'll perform clitoridectomies on every woman around the world.

End Uber Girl's hashtag bio.

'So Katherine, yes, Uber Girl is indeed a video game. But just any video game? No. How can ANYTHING be just ANYTHING when it has sold millions, billions worldwide? Uber Girl is at present the world's number one video game. Number one downloaded app. All that shit.'

Okay so let's have you stand up now, sir. Stand up to deliver the news that matters most to you first. Then the news that matters most to her after that.

'Katherine?'

'Yes,' she answers you.

'This Uber Girl movie?'

'Yes?'

'Guess who's a co-producer on it. C'mon guess? That's right me. Me. Me, me, me.'

Oh, what a fucking business this is, sir! There you are one day directing this semi low-budget Movie of the Week, maybe a few people on a bus in Turkey are ever going to see it, to, y voila, there you are, fuck man you're a co-producer on one of the hottest movies in development. All thanks to an old buddy of yours from film school who got you in. Ah, the movie biz, anything can happen and so often does.

So Katherine's mind is starting to turn. She congratulates you. Says,

'Zack that's great news. Great news. But what does this all have to do with me?'

Now come around to the front of your desk, sir. Come around. That's it. Now say it. Say it.

'Katherine it's unanimous all around. Among the bigwigs at the studio. Among the other producers. Among everyone who matters. You're it. You're the one. Uber Girl is Katherine Whitaker.'

Silence falls after that. Dead silence. You assume she's in shock. I mean what else would you assume? This means what? For her? The lead in a franchise, big studio movie. Huge exposure. Skyrocketing fame. Cash. Sequels. Seven to eight years of steady employment. Retire at thirty. She'll hit number 1 on the IMDB. Won't have to pay to put up her own pictures there anymore. Rip off.

'Now before it becomes all official Katherine you still must meet with the director. But don't sweat it, he doesn't have any pull. He's just this twentysomething kid. Made a few award winning shorts. Some commercials. The meeting is just a formality. To stroke his ego. Me and the other head honchos love to hire kids like this. It's so easy to boss them around.'

Katherine finally breaks her trance. Her silence. She starts nodding,

'Yes, yes, okay I'll meet with him. The director.' You say,

'Fabulous. Great. I'll set up a meeting with him next week. His name is MaCdee.'

Katherine looks at you dumbfounded.

'MaCdee? That's it? That's his name?'

'Hey listen sweetie if I find out he has another one I'll let you know, promise. Now let's get back to work.'

Now on your way out you say this to Katherine,

'Hey Katherine? You know the great thing about a movie like Uber Girl is that even if it's bad, it's still going to open, and open big. This is what happens when you cater to market first.'

'But what about catering to an audience first?'

'Well we're gonna try and do that too.'

All right so here we go getting back from lunch. Outside your office, sir, you congratulate Katherine, give her a hug, say,

'So proud of you sweetie. So proud of you.'

But wait a minute. Wait a minute. Katherine's mind isn't anywhere yours is right now.

TIGHT on Katherine's face.

SHE pulls away from the hug.

Now do a little abracadabra dissolve, abracadabra dissolve, so what's actually on her mind, we can see it. Abracadabra dissolve. Okay, see it. There it is. Laying there on the floor of the den. This thing that she discovered in the Armoire last night. Okay so zoom in on it. Zoom in on it very slowly. Very slowly. Okay stop. Everyone see it? Okay good.

DISSOLVE back to Katherine outside your office. Sir where have you gone? You must have fucked off somewhere. I don't know. This isn't about you right now, anyway, it's about Katherine. Katherine. Cue the Abracadabra dissolve again as she begins her walk. Screen starts to go fuzzy again. Fuzzy. Abracadabra dissolve. Abracadabra dissolve.

To Katherine's dream from last night. There she is, on her patio deck, checking out the view. The setting sun has almost set. Suddenly SOME GUY appears. Out of nowhere. In the blink of an eye. Total stud man. Hot. Leanly muscular. Now he's somewhere between the age of 32 and 42. Katherine can't be sure. His skin is dark, but not too dark. There's been some toning down here. Like let's say 300 to 400 years of interracial breeding to tone him down.

Katherine is checking him out, is impressed. Then, holy moly out of nowhere THE ARMOIRE suddenly appears, and our guy takes THE KEY. What key? THE KEY, the HAPPY and SAD faces key, and sticks it in the hole of the Armoire. He begins rummaging around, is digging deep amongst all those classic books, and, well, what do you know? He eventually pulls out a SCRIPT. A SCREENPLAY. A what? Yes. That's right. One of those things you make movies out of. He presents the script to Katherine. She accepts it. The two of them stare intensively at one another. (CU) CLOSE-UP of the front page. Katherine reads:

To Katherine Whitaker,

All my love,

Frank Cherbourg

Wait a minute? This guy is Frank Cherbourg? Thee Frank Cherbourg? The Francois Cherbourg from back in the day? Father of. . . .

Katherine looks up,

'But there is no title? Where is the title?' And from this we go to boom, bam, to the END OF THE DREAM.

KATHERINE is back on THE STUDIO LOT. She snaps out of her reverie real quick. The 3rd AD is in her ear.

'Katherine whenever you're ready, please head on over to makeup and hair for touch ups. Whenever you're ready. But if you're ready now, that would be great.'

Passive aggressive. Love it. Very Canadian.

And so here we are back in the studio. Back from lunch. The 1st Assistant Director is calling,

'1st team. Where's 1st team?'

Mabby's mother is there. The actress playing her that is. But where is Katherine? So unlike her to be late. Maybe she's still stuck in makeup and hair.

'No. She left us five minutes ago.'

'Okay where is she then?'

Ah, here she is. Here she is. Katherine enters.

'So sorry everyone. So sorry.' As she walks on over to you, sir, you notice that she looks pensive, deep in thought, not so much her happy go lucky self. Haven't we just told her she's going to play Uber Girl?

'I'm so sorry Zack. So sorry. My mind was wandering. I lost track of the time.'

'Where were you?'

'I was just outside, on my own. Thinking. You see, I was trying to remember the name of this thing that. . . .'

'The name of what?'

'The name. . . .'

And she stops herself short. All of a sudden her behavior has become very guarded. Protective. Then holy moly right out of the blue she says,

'I'm also having my period right now.'

And in deference we do stand to the wombs that bare us.

'No worries Sweetie.'

'All right.'

'Picture's up.'

'Picture's up everyone.'

Sir, you alert the troops.

'Listen everyone, we're only going to do this in one lens size. Katherine's coverage. Tightish. Head to shoulders. That's it and that's all, then we'll move on to whatever it is that we have planned for rest of the day. Copy?'

'Copy.'

'Katherine?'

'Yes?'

'Sweetie just give me what you gave me this morning in the master shot. That was good. Mabby, this girl that you're playing. She's very determined. Knows what she wants. This uncertain life, she's very certain about it. Follow your heart. Follow your dreams. Everyone should. That is until you wake up. Okay, someone ring the bell.'

'Ring the bell.'

'Picture's up.'

'Lock it up.'

'Quiet please.'

'Sound speed.'

'Sound is speeding.'

'All right roll camera.'

'Camera rolling.'

'Slate. Scene 26 take 1.'

'All right everyone. Quiet please. Settle. Settle.'

'Ladies ready? And action. . . .'

And off they go. The ladies start to act. Act, act, act. But sir something's the matter with Katherine. Her performance is off. Not that it's bad, it's just not good. The crew? Are they noticing? Nope. Now why would they be? The after lunch chocolate trolley has just come around, and everyone who can is stuffing their faces with chocolate.

Call cut? No, no. Let it play out. See what happens. Oops. Looks like Katherine has just forgotten her last line.

'What is it that you're doing with your life, young lady? What is it that you're doing?' her mother says. And Katherine was supposed to say,

'I'm doing what I believe in mother. That is all.'
'Cut.'

But Katherine couldn't remember it. Why?
'Cut.'

'That's a cut everyone.'

Bell rings. Doors fly open. People start chatting, reaching for more chocolate.

'Katherine?'

'Zack, I'm sorry. So sorry. I just. My mind went. . . .'

'Katherine don't worry about it. We'll just go again.'

'Going again.'

'Going again everyone.'

And weird? About her subpar, shitty performance, Katherine said not one word? Not one word. How odd? In the past she would have been all over her crappy acting before you could say anything. But not today. Hmm? Well the conclusion you draw from this is pretty obvious. Yes?

'Hey sweetie, maybe I should have waited until the end of the day to tell you about Uber Girl.'

'Uber Girl . . ? Uber Girl . . ? Oh, sure . . . Uber Girl.'

And, yes, insert a look of perplexity from you here sir.

'All right picture's up.'

'Here we go.'

'Ring the bell.'

'Sound speed.'

'Sound is speeding.'

'Roll camera.'

'Camera is rolling.'

'Slate. Scene 26 take 2.'

'All right, here we go. Ladies ready, and action. . . .'

Sir, take two is no different. Katherine is still way off. Doesn't look like she's feeling it at all. And the last line?

'I'm doing what I believe in mother. That is all.'

Forget it. She forgets it again. Stumbles all over it. Just goes completely blank. What the fuck is going on?

'Cut.'

'I'm so sorry. So sorry everyone. I don't know . . . I'll get it this time. Let's just go again.'

'Going again, right away.'

'Lock it up.'

One more take. Two more takes. Three more takes. Same thing. Same thing. Same thing. Geez, this is getting crazy. Okay, sir, why don't you step in and give her a little private pep talk? Good idea.

'Head outside for a coke and a smoke people.'

'Take five everyone.'

You approach Katherine.

'Sweetie what's the matter?'

'Can I be honest with you Zack? Here's why I keep drawing a blank on the last line. My mind goes to. . . .'

'To where does it go?'

'To . . . To . . . To this thing I found in the Armoire last night.'

And there it is. The look on her face. It's what you've been looking for, sir. You can't take your eyes off it. It's so captivating. So, so, so VITAL. Sir, you have an idea. A most brilliant idea.

'Katherine give me this. Give me what you're feeling right now. This girl Mabby really has a strong belief in what she's doing. Not up until now have I really seen this in you. When you mentioned this thing in the Armoire. What was this thing? This thing you discovered in there? It seems to have struck a chord with you. Touched you deeply, in a profound and personal way. You really believe in it. Want to follow it. Now don't tell me. Don't tell me what it is. I don't give a shit. What I do want you to do is this: Prepare emotionally on it. Meditate on whatever it was that you found in the Armoire before you start your scene. Capiche?'

Katherine begins nodding.

'And don't worry about the last line.'

'What?'

'Yeah, don't worry about it. Why not say whatever you want. Whatever is on your mind. The scripted line, we can just dub that in later. In post or whatever.'

'Okay.'

'All right. Picture's up.'

'Picture's up.'

'Ring the bell.'

'Sound speed.'

'Sound is speeding.'

'Roll camera.'

'Camera rolling.'

'Slate. Scene 26 take 6.'

'All right everyone settle. Settle.'

'And ladies, ready. And action.'

It worked. The scene is playing out beautifully. The crew, the look on their faces, they're transfixed with Katherine's performance. Even the most apathetic have put down their chocolates. And here it is. Here it comes, here it comes,

'What is it that you're doing with your life, young lady? What is it that you're doing?'

And Katherine says . . ?

'PELICULA. PELICULA is who I believe in. PELICULA is who I adore. PELICULA is who I want to follow.'

Katherine looks spent. Total silence abounds.

'Okay cut.'

'That's a cut.'

'All right, check the gate.'

'Check the gate.'

'If the gate is good we're moving on.'

'Gate is good.'

'All right, gate is good, so we're moving on over to the next studio.'

'Studio 1.'

'Copy that. Moving on over to studio 1.'

'Okay copy that.'

15

So you see Valued Reader, the truth about Pelicula is that she was never a girl to my mother. She was a script. A screenplay. Yes, one of those things you make movies out of. To my mother, you say? Yes. That's right. I am Wolfgang F. Whitaker. The son of Katherine Whitaker.

16

Now how this book finds its way to me Valued Reader is really inconsequential.

17

Oh for heaven's sake! Here is the truth of it all right here and right now. Valued Reader, I am Stand-in Guy. Stand-in Guy is me. I am the real author of this book. Never was there ever any Madeline Macdonald. Abigail Adams. Only in real life did these girls ever exist.

18

All right, so roll credits:

Care Facility Daughter. . . . .

Care Facility Son. . . . .

Mr. Trump. . . . .

24-Year-Old Katherine. . . . .

Katherine's Mother. . . . .

Badry Hungsobig. . . . .

Beggar Artist Strumming Guitar. . . . . . .

Abigail Adams. . . . .

Woman In Video Call. . . . .

Man In Video Call. . . . .

3rd AD. . . . .

1st AD. . . . .

Zack. . . . .

Joan Of Arc 1427. . . . .

Maddy. . . . .

Abby. . . . .

Mr. Big Cock King Kusi Obodum. . . . . .

Actress Playing Katherine's Mother. . . .

Anna K's Little Wanker Brother. . . .

Frank Cherbourg. . . . .

Sound Mixer. . . . .

Boom Operator. . . . .

Gaffer. . . . .

Grips. . . . .

DP. . . . .

Camera Operator. . . . .

114

Production Assistant. . . . .

Caterer #1. . . . .

AND INTRODUCING WOLFGANG F. WHITAKER as the son of Katherine Whitaker and Frank Cherbourg.

Yes. Yes. I am their son. And here's what else you need to know: It was about two years ago that I found this all out. Only two years. There I was, skimming the pages of my dead mother's diary, when, holy shit, my biological father is this dude named Cherbourg. What the fuck? Now instead of getting all whiny about this and checking into therapy I thought 'well why not go ahead and write a book about it?' So I did. And there you have it. A book about, me, my Mom and sundry other things. Anyway, here's the rest of what I know about her and Cherbourg: That their affair was a brief, but passionate five-day event. That she was still living in Cherbourg's house when it happened. That after the five days he buggered off and my mother never saw him again.

'I must leave you now Katherine,' he had said to her.

'To where Frank? To where are you going?'

'To Cape Coast Castle. In Africa. My great-great-great-great-grandmother is from there. Apparently from there. I won't be long. Maybe be gone for a month. To do some research for a new writing project. I'll call you as soon as I arrive. I promise.'

But he never called. Never got a chance to call cause he died shortly after his arrival. What? Yeah. There he was, checking out the castle, perusing one of the rooms where our ancestors used to chill, when some scaffolding came loose, collapsed on him, and killed him in an instant. Believe it Valued Reader. It's all in the diary.

And the script? Whatever happened to that? Pelicula. Who knows? Diary doesn't say. But maybe check for it underneath a floorboard somewhere. You know, if it's half as brilliant as my mother said it was then holy shit would it ever make for a good movie.

Oh and listen to this Valued Reader, this doozy, I almost forgot, the most important detail of all. Check THIS out. I mean imagine reading THIS in your mother's diary: Three months before Uber Girl was set to start shooting, contracts signed, all that shit, my mother found out she was pregnant. Pregnant with ME. Frank's baby. The baby from the affair. Isn't that crazy? Of course everyone around my mother thought she was nuts for saying yes to a baby and no to a movie.

'But Katherine. We don't understand? Why not have another baby when you're older? When you're done the franchise?'

'But I don't think you gentleman understand. It isn't any baby that I want. I want this baby.'

'But Katherine? Playing Uber Girl is an opportunity of a lifetime.'

'And having a baby isn't?'

So think about it Valued Reader. Had my mother gone on to star in a franchise movie, a movie she didn't really believe in. Taken the cash for cash's sake. Taken fame for fame's sake, then you would've never read any of this. Never read about the fictionalized lives of Madeline Macdonald and Abigail Adams (They were my dying mother's care aides in real life). Never have learned how I went about shafting Visa, MasterCard and American Express for all that money, so that I could bring this book to you. You would never have gone with me to the White Desert, met up with Badry Hungsobig and heard about all the chicks he got to tap. You would never have met my father Frank Cherbourg, paid a visit to his house, been into his den, seen the

Armoire, heard about the Happy and Sad Faces Key. The classic books. Pelicula. None of this would've happened had my mother gone on to play Uber Girl. Now, sure, I give a shit about all this Valued Reader, but do you?

19

'He was of mixed race.'
'But what a ridiculous choice of words!? We are all of mixed race. Of mixes nature knows not of.'

20

INT. STAND-IN GUY'S BACHELOR PAD
Wolfgang F. Whitaker (25), wearing a burgundy smoking jacket, sits at his desk, sipping a martini, while perusing his mother's diary. The manuscript for this book rests beside him. That he resembles the Frank Cherbourg we saw in Katherine's dream is uncanny. Eventually, he puts the diary down, GIVES a LOOK TO CAMERA, raises his glass, nods, then picks the diary up once again, returns to reading it.

> OKAY SO BOOK DONE. NOW WHO WANTS TO GO SEE THIS ON THE SCREEN?

Made in the USA
San Bernardino, CA
05 October 2017